To my Uncle Paul, a passionate golfer, and to my entire family for encouraging me on this adventure.

Copyright © 2024 by Debbie Hetmanek
Written by Debbie Hetmanek
Printed in the United States of America

All rights reserved. No part of this book may be used or reproduced in any manner whatsoever without the prior written permission of the author.
ISBN (Hardback): 979-8-9907767-0-8

Hello boys and girls!
Let's have fun golfing with Lolly and her grandson Frankie.

Every time you spot Buster in the story, shout BIRDIE!

Wow! This golf course looks so fun!
There are so many parts to explore.
Let's get started on those 18 holes.

Before Frankie goes golfing, he puts on his golf outfit and gets his clubs, balls, tees, water bottle, and yummy snacks.

Hole 1
The drive – bend, turn, and smash the driver! That's the big club.

Hole 2

A chip - a shot to get the ball onto the green or close to the hole. Some lucky chips go right into the hole.

Hole 3

A putt – a short, slow shot that rolls the ball into the hole.

The putter is Lolly's favorite club.

Hole 4
Frankie is keeping the score for each golfer. Lolly did not get a birdie.

Hole 5
See that big tree?
Lolly is aiming for it.

Hole 6

Oops! Lolly hit her ball into the sand. Frankie jumps in to get it. It sure is fun to play in.

Hole 8
No way! Is that an alligator?
Quick, run to the next hole.

Hole 9

Keep practicing and one day you could hit the ball really far like Frankie's best friend, his mommy. She won the longest drive!

Hole 10

Time for a snack. Frankie's favorites are apples and hot dogs.

Hole 11

Uh, oh! Mommy's shot went into the woods. Time to hit the ball back to the green grass (the fairway).

Hole 12

Lolly to the rescue to help Frankie chip the ball to the flag.

Hole 13

Drive the ball down the fairway, long and straight like Frankie's hero, his daddy.

Hole 14

Now it is Frankie's turn to hit the ball just like his daddy did!

Hole 15

Lolly was so happy to golf in Florence, Italy and make new friends. You can golf anywhere.

Hole 16

What in the world is going on here?

Frankie waits two minutes for the cows to move on.

Hole 17

Frankie rolls his ball right into the cup - a super duper putt. Time for a high five!

Hole 18
If you are very lucky and practice a lot, you could have a Hole-in-One like Lolly!

Goodbye boys and girls! I hope you learned a lot about golf from Lolly and Frankie.

Please be kind and always try your best!

Author's Note

I was thrilled to introduce my first grandchild, Frankie, to golf. One weekend when he was just 15 months old, I handed him toy plastic clubs and said, "Two hands, two hands" over one hundred times. By the end of the weekend, Frankie started to get the hang of it.

At age two, he was swinging the driver, chipper and putter. Frankie will enjoy saying "two hands" to cousin Meena and sister Evelyn in the next couple of years. Buster, a star in the book, is a statue that sits in Lolly's front yard. The illustrations in this book were inspired by Lolly's golf photographs of Frankie and her family. A special thank you for helping make this dream come true - my grandson Frankie, my daughter Carly, and her husband Josh.

About the Author

Debbie Hetmanek is a passionate golfer, a proud Virginia Tech Hokie, and an enthusiastic traveler to Italy. When with a grandchild, she never passes a carousel without enjoying a ride. Debbie lives with her husband in Vienna, Virginia. She adores her grandchildren who call her Lolly, and happily they live nearby.

Learn more at lollyslegacy.com

www.ingramcontent.com/pod-product-compliance
Lightning Source LLC
Chambersburg PA
CBRC091211010526
44119CB00020B/369